Acknowledgements

My dearest son Syon,
thank you for being my
happily ever after.

Published by S&B 2017
Copyright Sunita Shah and James Ballance
ISBN 978-1-78808-636-3

The Jai Jais

Ganesh

by Sunita Shah

Illustrated by James Ballance

Hello, my name is Ganesh.

I am a boy with an
elephant's head.

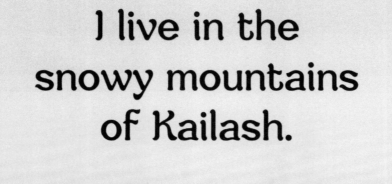

I live in the
snowy mountains
of Kailash.

I live with
my brother
Kartikeya.

My dad is called Lord Shiva.

He is a strong
and kind God.

He likes to break things!

My mum is called Parvati.

She is the Goddess of love.

I have a long trunk to
show you the right way.

I have big ears to
listen to what you say.

I have a big round tummy, which holds the whole universe!

I like to eat sweet laddoos
that are round and yummy.

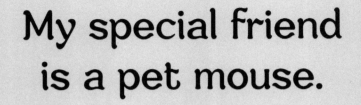

My special friend
is a pet mouse.

I travel on the mouse.

An elephant is a big
animal, and like me can
knock things out the way.

Little children pray to me to help them day to day.

Glossary

Kailash
- area with lots of mountains in the south west region of Tibet.

Laddoo
- ball-shaped sweets made of flour and sugar, which are eaten at festivals.